# AILA™
### Sit & Play

# Read Aloud Stories

A Library of 60 Storybooks All Included in the
AILA™ Virtual Preschool Learning System

DMAI

*AILA™ Sit & Play Read Aloud Stories*

TM & © 2020 DMAI, Inc. All rights reserved.  AILA™, Animal Island™, and all related titles, logos, and characters are trademarks of DMAI, Inc.

Printed in China

ISBN 978-1-7353344-0-0

## Tips for Reading with Your Child

Before you begin, announce how many stories you'll be reading together. Afterwards, share your thoughts and encourage your child to share as well. There's a good chance your child won't want storytime to end!

Here are a few more helpful tips to make storytime a rewarding experience:

• The stories in this book can be read in any order, so feel free to skip around.

• Try taking turns choosing which stories to read.

• Ask your child questions about the story and point out things in the art.

• For fun, try acting out the character voices!

• With older children, point out the title, author, and words as you read.

Most of all ... have fun and enjoy your time together!

## How to Use this Book

Read the story pages from top-to-bottom, left-to-right.

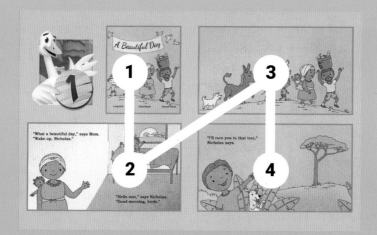

# Contents
Alphabetical Order

# A Beautiful Day

*Lindy Pelzl*  *Elana Bregin*  *Raeesah Vawda*

"What a beautiful day," says Mom.
"Wake up, Nicholas."

"Hello sun," says Nicholas.
"Good morning, birds."

"It's a lovely day," says Dad.
"Let's have a picnic by the river."

"Can my friend Jacob come?"
asks Nicholas.

"Don't forget me. I love picnics!"
says Donkey.

"And me. I want to come too!"
says Dog.

"Follow us,"
say the birds.

"I'll race you to that tree,"
Nicholas says.

"I won, I won," says Donkey.

"Not fair," says Nicholas.
"You've got four legs."

"Look what I can do,"
says Nicholas.

"I bet you can't do this,"
says Jacob.

"Here's our picnic spot,"
says Dad.

"Race you to the water!"
says Jacob.

"Come and eat, boys and girls,"
says Mom.

"Time to go home," says Mom.
"Say goodbye to Jacob."

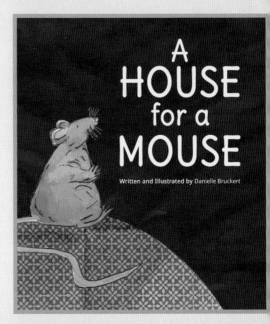

# A HOUSE for a MOUSE

Written and Illustrated by Danielle Bruckert

Mouse was looking for a new house.

This looks like a nice house.

"You can come and sleep with me,"
said Puppy.

"Thank you," said Mouse.

That night, Mouse's dreams were
bouncy and muddy.

"You can come and sleep with me,"
said Parrot.

"Thank you," said Mouse.

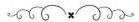

That night, Mouse's dreams
were noisy and wild.

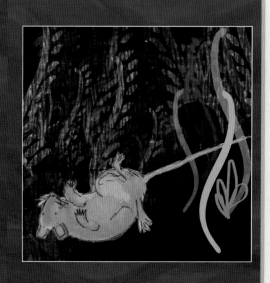

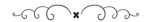

"You can come and sleep with me,"
said Fish.

"Thank you," said Mouse.

That night, Mouse's dreams were cold and wet.

Mouse needed somewhere warm and dry.

Mouse found a bookshelf nearby.

That night, Mouse had warm and cozy dreams.

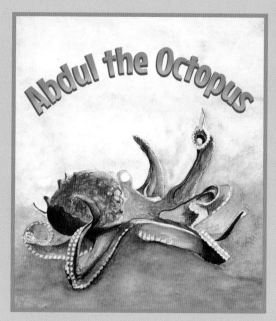

# Abdul the Octopus

Hi there!
I am Abdul
the Octopus.

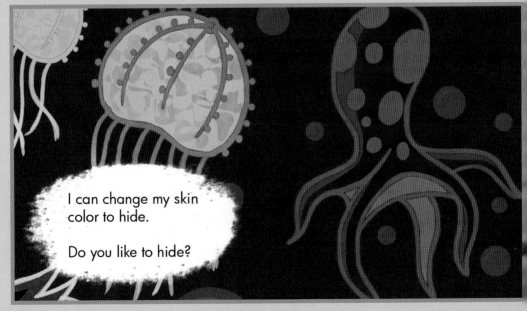

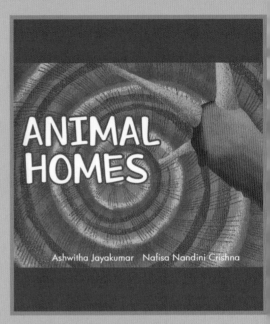

# ANIMAL HOMES

Ashwitha Jayakumar    Nafisa Nandini Crishna

Animals live all around us.

Birds build
their homes
up high.

And so do bees.

Spiders spin their homes.

Tiny termites build
tall, tall homes.

Snails and tortoises grow homes on their backs.

Fish live in the water. Frogs can live in water and on land.

Rabbits and rats live in burrows under the ground.

Monkeys and apes make trees their homes.

Bears and wolves
live in dens.

Crocodiles live in swamps.

30

Deer live in forests and so do tigers!

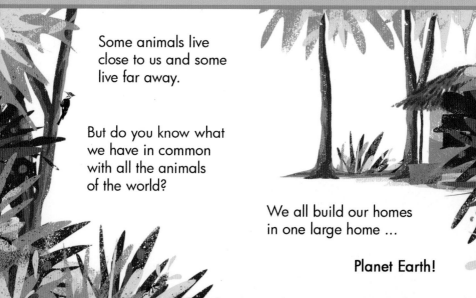

Some animals live close to us and some live far away.

But do you know what we have in common with all the animals of the world?

We all build our homes in one large home ...

**Planet Earth!**

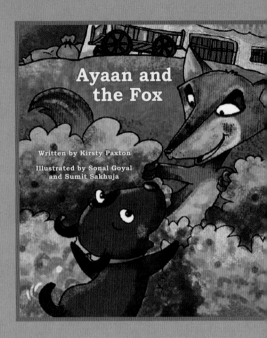

**Ayaan and the Fox**

Written by Kirsty Paxton

Illustrated by Sonal Goyal and Sumit Sakhuja

There once was
a little dog named Ayaan.

Ayaan was asleep,
but the moon was awake.

"Wake up," said the moon.
Ayaan woke up.

"Have you seen my friend, Fox?" asked Ayaan.

"No," said the moon.

"I will go and look for him," said Ayaan.

Ayaan saw cows.

Ayaan saw pigs.

Ayaan saw a little cat.

But he did not see a fox.

Ayaan met an owl.

"Where is Fox?" he asked.

"Look in the pink tree," said the owl.

Ayaan met a bat under the pink tree.

"Where is Fox?" he asked.

"Look in the purple tree," said the bat.

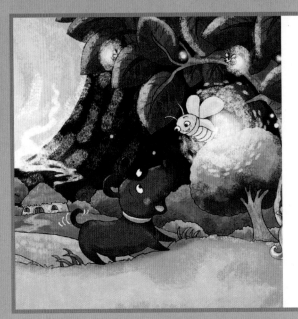

Ayaan met a firefly
at the purple tree.

"Where is Fox?" he asked.

"Look in the grass,"
said the firefly.

Ayaan met a cricket
in the grass.

"Where is Fox?" he asked.

"Look in the green tree,"
said the cricket.

Ayaan looked in the green tree, but the fox was not there.

Ayaan could not find Fox anywhere.

Fox jumped out from behind a bush.

"Surprise!" he said.

"Hello Fox," said Ayaan. "Nobody knew where you were."

"Yes we did!" said the owl, and the bat, and the firefly, and the cricket
"We tricked you."

Ayaan laughed.

"You did trick me!"
he said.

"Now, who wants to play?"

44

WOW!

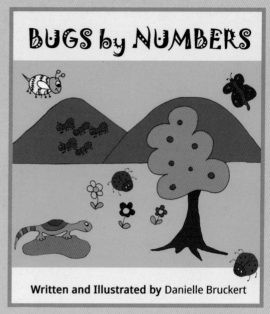

# BUGS by NUMBERS

**Written and Illustrated by** Danielle Bruckert

Down in the garden
under the tree,
there's a whole lot of creatures
living with me.

Down in the garden
under the tree,
how many GECKOS
can you see?

ONE!

One colorful GECKO,
lying happily.

Down in the garden
under the tree,
how many BUZZY BEES
can you see?

# 2
## one, TWO!

Two BUZZY BEES
flying freely by me.

Down in the garden
under the tree,
how many LADY BUGS
can you see?

# 3

## ONE, TWO, THREE!

Three LADY BUGS
playing daintily.

Down in the garden
under the tree,
how many BUTTERFLIES
can you see?

# 4
## one, two, three
## FOUR!

Four beautiful BUTTERFLIES
fluttering by me.

Down in the garden
under the tree,
how many ARMY ANTS
can you see?

**5**
one, two, three,
four, FIVE!

Five angry ARMY ANTS,
marching two by three.

ONE gecko;
TWO buzzy bees;
THREE ladybugs;
FOUR butterflies;
FIVE army ants.

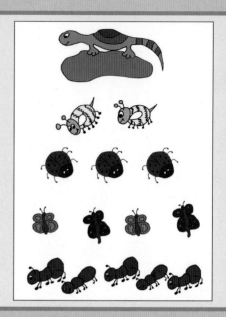

These are all the creatures
living with me,
down in the garden,
under the tree.

# Busy Ants

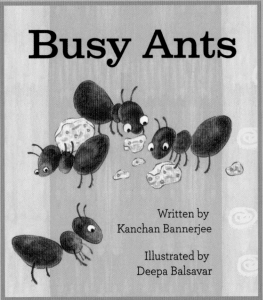

Written by
Kanchan Bannerjee

Illustrated by
Deepa Balsavar

Hello.

I am the fourth one in the line.

Can you see me?

Left, right, left, right.
We walk silently in a line.

I just got an idea.
I am going to get a set of

# WHEELS

to move faster!

We are not noisy like other animals.

Ours is a language of **smells**.

One kind of smell says,

**"follow
me
this
way
for
a
feast."**

Another smell says,
**"Danger!
Do not go there."**

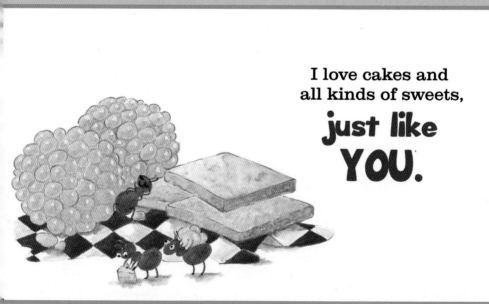

I love cakes and
all kinds of sweets,
**just like
YOU.**

Want to see my
muscles at work?

I may look very tiny to you,
but I am very

**STRONG.**

Never mind if
the door is shut.

I can slip through
the smallest
crack.

Believe it or not, hundreds of us live happily in a **COLONY.**

# Clever Pig

Written by Nathalie Koenig
Ilustrated by Josh Morgan

Come Pig! Let's play.

Can you find the carrot?

No, it's not under there.

No, it's not inside.

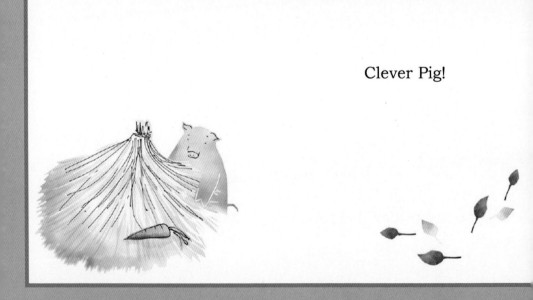

Clever Pig!

Wake up, Pig!
Come out and play.

Where is she?

Pig is gone.

The sun came up.

And the sun
went down.
But no Pig.

I miss my friend.

My Pig! Clever Pig.

And one ... two ...          ... three new friends!

Come, pigs!

Let's play!

Time for bed!

Goodnight, pigs.

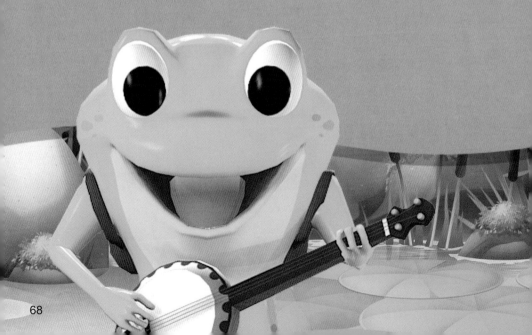

# COLORS!

**Written by** Justin Amey    **Illustrated by** Jesse Breytenbach

**Translated by** Lea Shaver

Look! A rainbow!

**This is red.**

What is red here?

**His shirt**
**His shorts**
**Her dress**

# This is orange.

**What is orange here?**

A cat
A fish
Her dress
Oranges
The cabinets
The wall

## This is yellow.

## What is yellow here?

A flower
An egg
A banana
Her dress

# This is green.

## What is green here?

**The plants**
**The frog**
**Her dress**

73

**This is blue.**

**What is blue here?**

The sky
The birds
Her dress

# This is indigo.

What is indigo here?

**The berries**
**Her jacket**
**Her dress**

# This is violet.

What is violet here?

The flowers
The sky
Her dress

What colors do you see?

**The End**

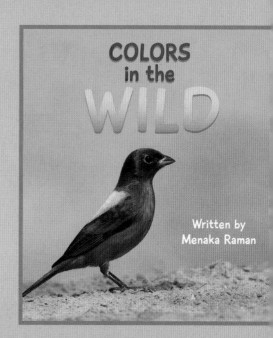

COLORS
in the
WILD

Written by
Menaka Raman

The parrot is green.

The elephant is gray.

The bear is black.

The flamingos are pink.

The butterfly is orange.

What colors do
you see here?

COLORS of NATURE

I see a blue butterfly waving goodbye.

I see a yellow bee
drinking a cup of tea.

I see a red fish in a dish.

I see a green frog
playing with a puppy dog.

I see an orange duck
wishing me good luck.

I see a violet flower
dancing with a caterpillar.

I see a gray and black cat
wearing an orange hat.

I see a gray and brown mouse
hiding in a pink house.

I see a red and black fox
wearing purple socks.

I see a green grasshopper reading a black and white newspaper.

I see a black and purple goat sailing in a red boat.

I see
a green and brown crocodile
giving me a big smile.

I see
a black and blue snake
eating a slice of cake.

I see a red and yellow hen writing with a pen.

I see a black and orange tiger standing in the water.

I see with my two black eyes
all the colors as they fly.

The End

# Come stay with Me

Nasrin Siege    Job Mubinya

Tendai Turtle lives in the water.

Tendai's best friend is Bunny Busi.
She lives in a tree.

Granny Turtle has hurt her shell.

"We have to go to help Granny" says Mom.

"You can come stay with me, Tendai!" calls Busi.

Tendai stays with
Bunny Busi in the tree.

They play all day.

They sleep all night.

The next day Mom and Dad come back with Granny.

"How are you, Granny?" asks Tendai.

"I am better now, " says Granny with a smile.

"We fixed her shell," answers Mom.

Granny gives Tendai her favorite flute.

Tendai plays the flute,
and everybody dances.

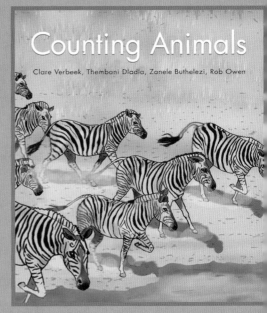

# Counting Animals

Clare Verbeek, Thembani Dladla, Zanele Buthelezi, Rob Owen

One elephant is going to drink water.

Two giraffes are going to drink water.

Three buffaloes and four birds are also going to drink water.

99

Five antelopes and six warthogs are walking to the water.

Seven zebras are running to the water.

Eight frogs and nine fish
are swimming in the water.

One lion roars.
He also wants to drink.
Who is afraid of the lion?

One elephant is drinking water with the lion.

# FRIENDS

Illustrated by: Catherine Groenewald

My name is Simo.

I have four friends.

Their names are
Zizo, Lele, Sisa
and Ayanda.

My friend Zizo
likes to play soccer.

My friend Lele
likes to swim.

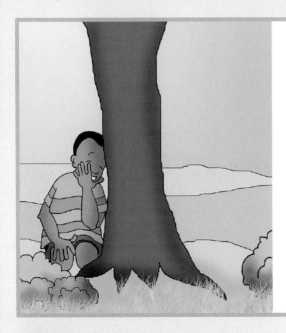

My friend Sisa
likes to play
hide-and-seek.

My friend Ayanda
likes to read.

Me? I like to
do the things
they like to do.

I play soccer
with Zizo.

I swim with Lele.

I play hide-and-seek with Sisa.

Come, friend.
What do you like?

Come play soccer
with us.

Come swim with us.

Come play hide-and-seek with us.

Come read with us!

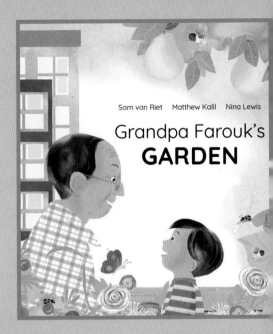

Sam van Riet    Matthew Kalil    Nina Lewis

# Grandpa Farouk's GARDEN

Deep in the city is where you'll find Grandpa Farouk's garden

Amir visits Grandpa
once a week.

He loves the leaves and
flowers and trees.

He helps with the compost too.

Amir helps to water the plants.

When all the work in the garden is done, Amir and Grandpa feast on a harvest of fruit.

One day, Grandpa doesn't eat his pear.
"What's wrong?" asks Amir.

"My garden is unwell," says Grandpa.
"Look closely. Tiny pests are eating the plants," says Grandpa.

"We need ladybugs!
They will eat up all the pests!"

"I can bring you ladybugs,"
says Amir.

And he does!

Amir finds one ladybug on
the sports field.

He finds two more at the shop,

three at the park ...

Amir takes the ladybugs to Grandpa Farouk.
"Well done! You found 10 ladybugs!" says Grandpa

... and four behind the TV.

Grandpa is very happy.
The ladybugs fly into
the garden.

And the garden blossoms.

The garden is full of flowers again.
"Thank you, ladybugs!" says Amir.

118

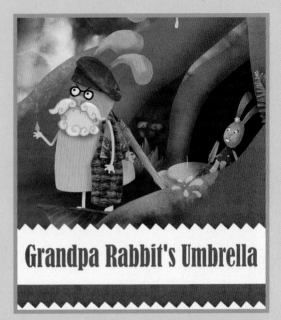

## Grandpa Rabbit's Umbrella

There was a storm coming, and Grandpa Rabbit needed his umbrella to collect more carrots.

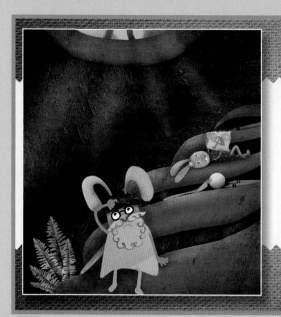

"Where is my umbrella?" he said, going through the rabbit home and searching for it.

"I'm sure it can't be far away."

"Perhaps it is in the washing pile!" he said, diving into the basket.

"Perhaps I put it in
the food bag by mistake,"
he said, turning the bag
upside down.

"Flopsy," said Grandpa Rabbit.
"I'll give you a carrot if you
find my umbrella."

"Ok!" said Flopsy.

Grandpa Rabbit climbed the bookshelves and searched behind every book.

The other rabbits looked on, worried, as Grandpa searched each book individually.

"I don't think it's here," said Grandpa Rabbit.

"Maybe I left it outside,"
he said, as Flopsy helped him.

"Maybe it is hidden in
the carrots or in storage,"
he said.

"Well done, Flopsy!" said Grandpa Rabbit, as she took the umbrella off his back.
"You get a carrot for finding it!"

Grandpa opened the umbrella and went into the rain, waving the rabbits goodbye as he went in search of more carrots.

And Flopsy sneaked along to help Grandpa.
"Right, let's get some more carrots!" said Grandpa.
"Now, where is my umbrella?"

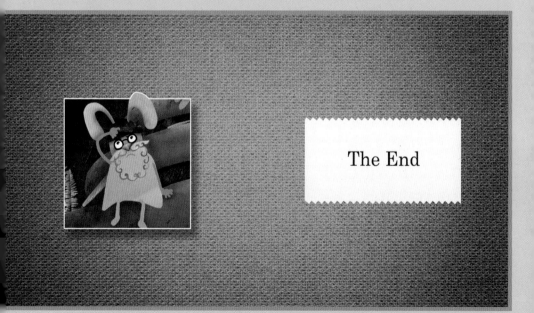

The End

Jennie Marima    Imile Wepener    Rox Jaden Palmer

My name is Lolo.
I have many friends.
Come out with me
to say hello!

Hello Sun,
big and bright.
You fill the day
with your bright light.

Hello Grass,
soft and green.
You give us all
a place to play.

Hello Sky,
broad and blue.
You fill the sky
with the color blue.

Hello Moon,
up in the dark.
You make the night
not so dark.

Hello Star,
big and white.
You make the night
so very nice.

Hello Wind,
strong and free.
You blow things around,
and make it cool.

Hello Rain,
pouring down.
You bring water,
and cool our ground.

Hello Lightning,
from high above.
Your bright flashing light
gives us a fright.

Hello Thunder,
roaring in the rain.
You make a boom noise,
so very loud.

Hello Dew,
drops of water.
You make the groud
soft and wet.

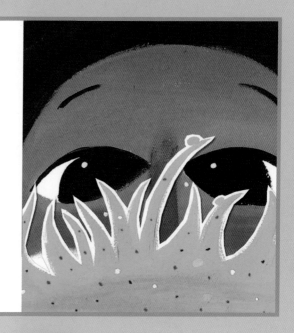

Hello Tree,
big and strong.
You give us shade
and fruit to eat.

Hello Bird,
flying in the sky.
You fill our days
with lovely songs.

Hello You,
reading this book.

Now you've met my friends,
please show me yours!

# Hello Seal, Will You Play With Me?

By Zehnya Bruckert

Hello, seal.

You look so cute.

Will you play with me today?

Hello, friendly seal.
You look so friendly.
Will you play with me today?

Hello, elephant seal.
Your nose is so big.
Can you smell well?
Would you like to play with me today?

Hello, baby seal.

You look so young and new.

Will your mom let you play with me?

Hello curious seal,

You look so curious. What do you want to ask?

And, would you like to play today?

Hello spotty seal,
You look so spotty.
Will you play with me
today?

Hello, silly seal.
You look silly with
your tongue out.
Will my mom let me
play with you today?

Hello, fluffy seal.
You look so fluffy.
Will you play with me today?

Hello, shark.
You look scary.
I don't think I should play with you today.

137

Hello, sleepy seal.
You look so sleepy.
Should we play,
or should we sleep?

It's time for me to go
to bed.
Goodbye, seals.
I hope we can play
again tomorrow!

Mom, can I take this seal with me to bed?

# Hide and Seek

Doug plays hide-and-seek with his mom.

He finds seven baskets.

Six vases.

Five badminton birdies.

Four pairs of pants.

Three musical instruments.

Two hands.

143

One mom!

# How Do You Feel?

Menaka Raman

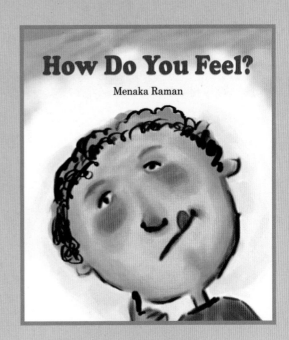

Happy?

Giggly?

Lonely?

Angry?

 Irritated?

Sad?

Worried?

149

How are you
feeling today?

150

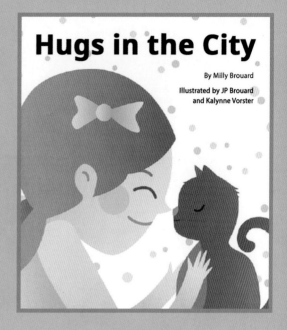

# Hugs in the City

By Milly Brouard

Illustrated by JP Brouard
and Kalynne Vorster

My name is Jilly.

Today, I hugged most of the cats in town!

I hugged the neighbor's cat, Ben.

**MEOW?**

Ben said "Meow?"

I hugged the cat who lives under the bench in the park.

He squiggled, and he wriggled.

I hugged Mrs. Lilly's tubby ginger cat.

He licked my face.
"Slurp, slurp, slurp."
**SLURP!**

153

I hugged the cat
who eats outside
the fish and chips shop.

He went, "Om nom nom."

I even hugged
the grumpy cat
who doesn't like hugs!

He yowled and yowled.

I hugged a short cat.

I hugged a long cat.

I hugged an old cat.

I hugged a young cat.

I hugged a mommy cat,            and every kitten she had.

I tried to hug the big cats
at the zoo ...

... but the zookeeper said,
**"NO!"**

I climbed on the bus
and hugged the cat
that was hiding in
an old lady's bag.

The old lady
shrieked!

**SHRIEK!**

I went home and got into bed.

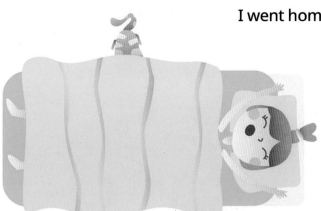

**YAWN!**

Some furry things snuck in ...

...and hugged me.

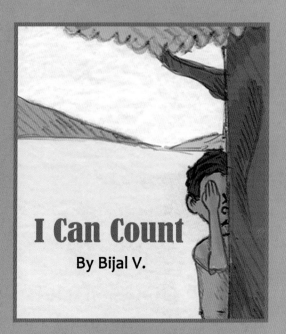

# I Can Count
## By Bijal V.

One owl goes            *Hoot*

Two dogs snore     *Khrrr  Khrrr*

Three tigers say    *Aaahun  Aaahun  Aaahun*

160

# Four lions growl

*Grrr  Grrr  Grrr  Grrr*

# Five frogs say

*Croak  Croak  Croak
Croak  Croak*

## Six flamingoes say

*Honk  Honk  Honk*
*Honk  Honk  Honk*

## Seven zebras say

Haw  Haw  Haw  Haw
Haw  Haw  Haw

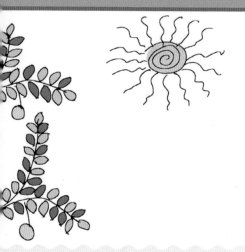

# Eight deer say

*Auuu  Auuu  Auuu  Auuu*
*Auuu  Auuu  Auuu  Auuu*

# Nine fish go

*Splish  Splish  Splish  Splish  Splish*
*Splish  Splish  Splish  Splish*

# Ten people say

*One*
*Two*
*Three*
*Four*
*Five*
*Six*
*Seven*
*Eight*
*Nine*
*Ten*

# I Like to Read

By Letta Machoga

Illustrated by Wiehan de Jager

I like to read.

Who can I read to?

My sister is asleep.

Who can I read to?

My mother and grandmother are busy.

Who can I read to?

My father and
grandfather are busy.

Who can I read to?
I can read to myself!

# I Will Help You

Andrea Abbott     Olivia Villet     Fathima Kathrada

"Ouch!"
Mama Heron hurts her
wing and leg on barbed wire.

"I am hurt.
I can't get home to my children."

"Please help me."

"Why are you crying,
Mama Heron?"

"I can't get home
to my children."

"I will help you," says Lungile.

"Thank you, Lungile!"

On the way, he stops to play with his friends in the river.

The next day, Grandmother sends Lungile to the shop to buy bread.

Uh-oh! The money is gone.

"Don't come home until
you find that money!"
says Grandmother.

"Why are you crying, Lungile?"

"I lost the money Grandmother
gave me to buy bread.
We have no supper now."

"I will help you."

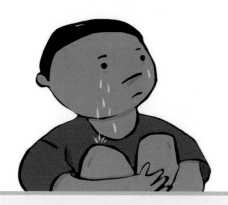

Mama Heron's sharp eyes
see the coins shining
in the water.

"Thank you, Mama Heron."

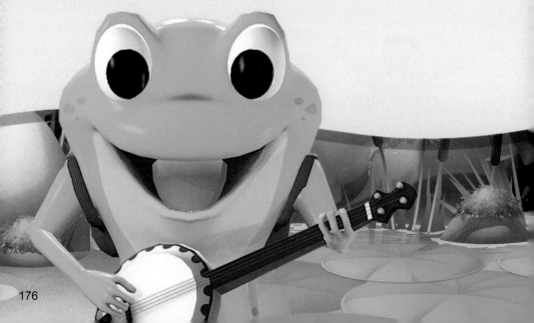

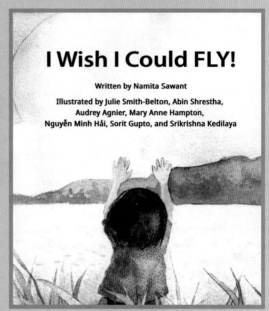

# I Wish I Could FLY!

**Written by Namita Sawant**

**Illustrated by Julie Smith-Belton, Abin Shrestha,
Audrey Agnier, Mary Anne Hampton,
Nguyễn Minh Hải, Sorit Gupto, and Srikrishna Kedilaya**

I wish I could fly ...
up and up in the sky!

I would roll to the clouds.

I would rest on
the highest treetop.

I would fly to the beach and play.

Then, I will fly and eat
my favorite ice cream.

Garden, mountains, fields, jungle, stars and moon ...

I wish I could fly ...
wherever I love to!

It's Rahah's birthday next week. She's excited about inviting her new friends to her party.

"Who will you invite?" asks Mom. "You've only been at school a few months. The kids all seem so very different, don't they?"

"No, Mom. I have lots of new friends," says Rahah.

"I want to invite Zerina. She wants to be a ballerina, just like me!"

"Oh lovely," says Mom.
"We'll play some dance music."

"I hope that Sikelele can come too. He sings in the school choir, just like me."

"Oh that's good," says Mom. We'll all have fun singing."

"Can we invite Susheela? She's got fluffy kittens, just like me."

"Yes," says Mom.
"She'll have fun playing
with our kittens too."

"And we must invite Yongnam.
She loves pink cupcakes even
more than I do."

"It's lucky I'm making cupcakes then," says Mom.

"She can have the pink ones."

"Thanks, Mom! I can't wait."
"Oh Rahah! I'm so excited to meet all your friends. They sound so special—just like you!"

"But what about you?
You love books, don't you...
just like me!

Would you like to come
to my party too?"

## Lara the Yellow Ladybug

Lara the ladybird was a special bug.

Unlike all her friends, she had bright yellow wings.

Everyone loved her yellow wings.

Each morning, Bibi Butterfly said hello.
And Manto Mantis always waved.

Even Sesa, the sulky spider,
was happy to see her.

At school, she played with lots of friends.

But Lara wanted to be like the other ladybirds.

"I wish I had red wings like you, Mama," she cried.

So one day, to cheer her up, Lara's mother painted her wings bright red.

The next morning, nobody greeted Lara on her way to school.

And when she got there, none of her friends said hello.

Lara sat all alone.
No one noticed
her new red wings.

Until Miss Miya spotted her and said: "You've painted your lovely yellow wings!"

Lara's classmates were shocked.
"Your wings are special!"
"So unique!"
"So rare!"

"Lara," Miss Miya said, "your yellow wings are what make you you.
Like Sipho's spot...
and Sally's legs."

Back home, Lara took a long bath and scrubbed until her golden wings gleamed.

"I'll never paint my wings again!"
she thought. Except, maybe once or twice …

To try a bit of purple
… or something nice.

But not for ever and
just for fun.

# Let's Eat a Rainbow!

I see a rainbow we can eat.

# Look!

a red strawberry

a pink grapefruit

an orange pumpkin

a yellow lemon

a green pea

a blueberry

a purple cabbage

a white cheese

a brown loaf
of bread

and a black bean.

We will need
more to share.

We will need ...

red strawberries

## pink grapefruits

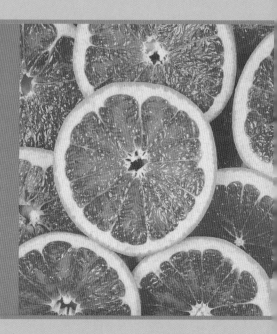

## orange pumpkins

yellow lemons

green peas

**blueberries**

**purple cabbages**

white cheeses

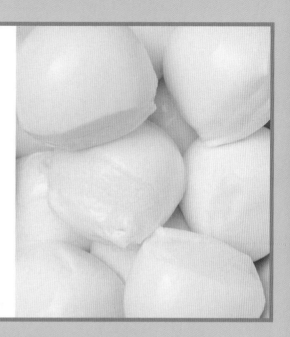

brown loaves
of bread

and black beans.

# Let's Have An Inside Day!

Lerato Mbangeni    Alicia van Zyl

Let's have an inside day!

A pancake, syrup, and berries day.

A jump on the bed and twirling day.

A dress up like dad
and take pictures day.

Let's have an
inside games day.

But whisper when we pass Mama's room.

Let's have a dancing and singing day.

A tickle tummies and eat gummies day.

Let's get snuggly and tell stories. Fall asleep and get snoring ...

Because an inside
day is a busy day.

# Little Goat

Nicola Anne Smith    Tiffany Mac Sherry    Mirna Lawrence

Little Goat went to find the sweetest grass.

The sky was blue above.
But she did not look up.

The river gurgled below.

But Little Goat did not listen to its song.

A bird called to her, saying, "How do you do?"

But Little Goat didn't answer.

She just walked along
looking for the sweetest grass.

As she walked along, Little Goat
moved further and further away
from Mother Goat.

Little Goat found
the sweetest grass.
She ate and ate.

She had walked far from
Mother Goat.

Mother Goat wondered
where Little Goat had gone.

She looked in the mealie patch,
but Little Goat was not there.

Mother Goat ran to the river.
But Little Goat was not there.
"Where are you, Little Goat,"
bleated Mother Goat.

A bird called to Mother Goat.
"Little Goat is asleep in the
sweet grass across the bridge."

220

Mother Goat crossed the bridge,
to the sweet grass.

There she found Little Goat
fast asleep.

"Wake up, Little Goat,"
said Mother Goat gently.
"You were lost!

"I wasn't lost ... I have been here
all the time!" said Little Goat.

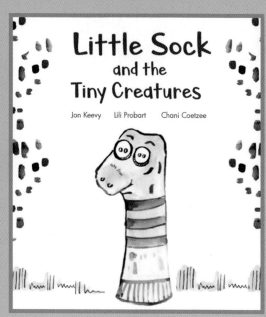

# Little Sock
## and the
## Tiny Creatures

Jon Keevy    Lili Probart    Chani Coetzee

It's wash day for the Socks.

# OH NO!

Little Sock falls out!

"I have to get home," says Little Sock.

"Do you know the way home?" asks Little Sock.

"No, but take this,"
says the Robot.

"Do you know the way home?"
asks Little Sock.

"No, but take this,"
says the Mouse.

"Do you know the way home?"
asks Little Sock.

"No, but take ...                    OOPS!"

"Maybe the marble knows
the way home," says Little Sock.

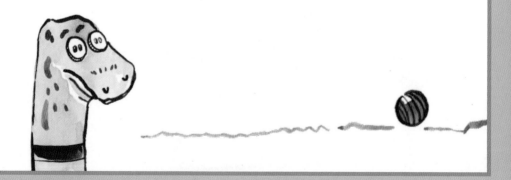

"It does!"
says Little Sock.

Little Sock is happy.

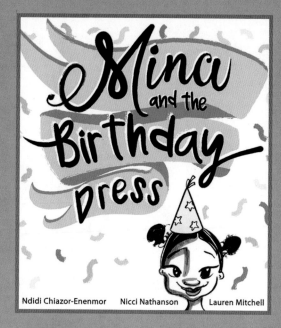

Mina and the Birthday Dress

Ndidi Chiazor-Enenmor    Nicci Nathanson    Lauren Mitchell

Tomorrow is Mina's birthday. She is having a party in the garden.

Mina is going to the shops with Mom to buy a birthday dress.

"I want a blue dress," Mina says.

Mom finds a lovely blue dress.

Mina shakes her head.
"I don't want a blue dress."

"I want a pink dress,"
Mina says.

Mom shows her a
beautiful pink dress.

Mina folds her arms.

"I don't want a pink dress."

"I want a green dress," Mina says.

Mom holds out a pretty green dress.

Mina frowns.

"I don't want
a green dress."

Mom says, "You don't want
a blue dress, you don't want
a pink dress, and you don't
want a green dress."

"What about this dress?"

Mina says,
"Yes! I love yellow.
I want the yellow dress."

# My Best Friend

By Anupa Lal       Illustrated by Suvidha Mistry

I have a friend. She lives in my house.

When I am happy, so is she.

When I cry, she cries too.

But I cannot hear her voice. My friend lives inside the mirror.

"Come out," I tell her. "We will play." She does not come out.

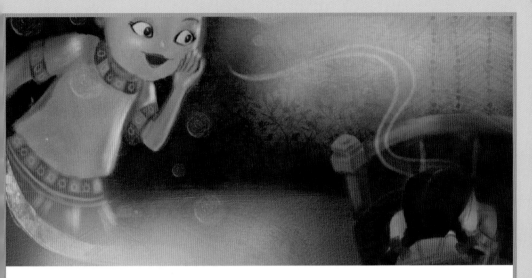

I am not happy. I go to sleep.

She comes out of the mirror in my sleep! And we have fun.

We play, we run, we shout and scream together.

When I talk to her, she also talks to me.

In the morning, my friend will go back into the mirror.

But I don't mind at all. We will play again in my dreams!

# My Brother and Me

Written by Kanchan Bannerjee
Illustrated by Pallak Goswamy

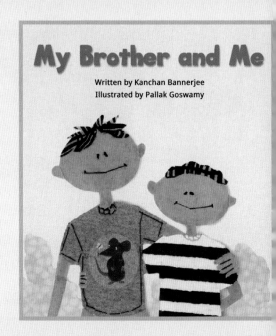

This is Sam.
He is in fourth grade.

This is me.
I am in first grade.

Every morning,
we get ready for school.

I can button my **shirt**.

**shirt**

Sam helps me put on my
**shoes and socks**.

**shoes and socks**

Sam puts me on his **bike**.

bike

Sam reads big **books**.

books

I carry a small **bag**.

**bag**

After school, Sam plays soccer.
He kicks the **ball**.

**ball**

Sam scores a **goal**!

**goal**

After soccer,
he buys me **ice cream**.

**ice cream**

It is five o'clock.
It's time to go **home**.

**home**

247

Kanchan Bannerjee    Pratyush Gupta

# My Chintu

This dog has small ears.          This dog has big ears.

248

This dog is white.

This dog is black.

This dog has a
long, pointy face.

This dog has a
short, flat face.

This dog is very quiet.

This dog is very loud!

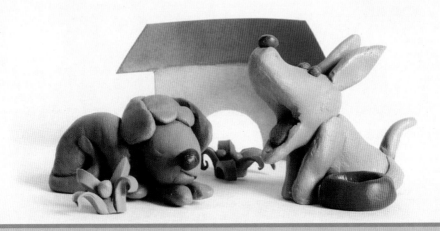

Look at this dog!
This dog is helpful.
This dog is playful.
This dog is cheerful.
This is a very special dog.

This is my Chintu.

# THE END

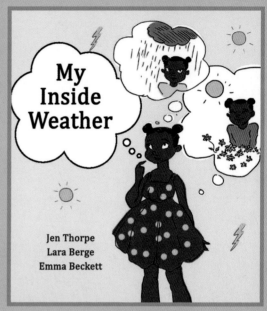

# My Inside Weather

Jen Thorpe
Lara Berge
Emma Beckett

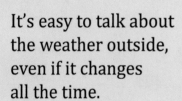

It's easy to talk about the weather outside, even if it changes all the time.

But it's hard to talk about the weather inside me. Sometimes it feels like people don't understand.

Do you feel like that too?

Some days my mind is full of sunshine and rainbows. I feel like I can do anything.

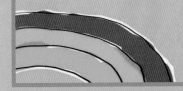

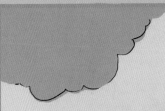

On other days, my head is full of fog and clouds. It's hard to listen to what people are saying or to remember things.

I sometimes wake up
feeling like it's windy
and wild in my head.
I feel tired and grumpy.

And sometimes, it feels
like it's raining inside me.
It can be a drizzle making
me feel sad, or a storm
making me feel angry.

Sometimes, the weather inside me doesn't match the weather outside.

Sometimes, my inside weather doesn't match how I want to feel or how I think I should feel.

Is that okay?

Yes, of course it is.

The best thing to do
when we feel like our
inside weather is strange
is to tell someone we love,
and talk about it.

They've got
inside weather too,
and they'll understand.

# My Red Ball

Ball.

My ball.

My red ball.

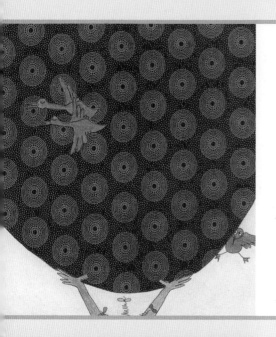

My big red ball.

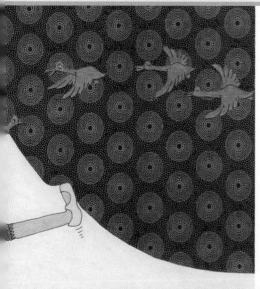

I kick.

I kick my ball.

I kick my red ball.

I kick my red ball
hard!

Where?

Where is my ball?

Where is my ball now?

Where is my red ball now?

It is up.

It is high up.

It is high up in the sky.

It is high up in the sky.

It is over the moon.

It is gone!

Melissa Fagan    Kobie Nieuwoudt

My Special Blankie

Can you see me?

I'm on Mama's back
in my special blankie.

I love Mama.
And Mama loves me.

And I love, love, LOVE
my special blankie.

Bang!

Boom!

Bash!

I like to make a noise.

But Mama likes quiet.

Mama does her work.

271

But when I eat, Mama says my special blankie must watch.

And when I wash, my special blankie must wait where it is dry.

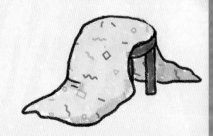

I love bedtime
stories with Mama.

My special blankie
listens with me ...

.. and helps
me go to sleep.

I love, love, LOVE
my special blankie.

Liora Friedland    Karen Vermeulen    Melissa Visser

Nosisi, it's time to stop playing.

Please come inside.

Look at these beautiful butterflies.

*No!*

Come help Mama make some rice.

*No!*

Let's feed Shakes.

No!

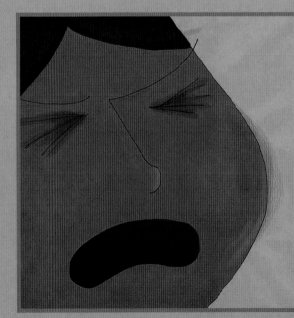

Nosisi, it's bath time ...

No!

No

No

No

*No!*

Nonononono ...

How about an ice cream?

*No!*

279

Oh.
Not no ...

Yes!

Yummy. Yummy.

Yay!

Yay!

Yay!

Nosisi, will you tidy your room?

Hmmmm. Okay!

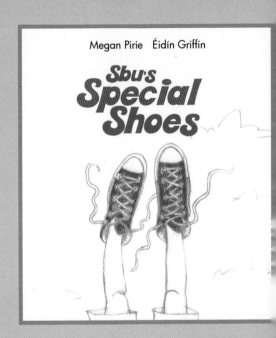

Megan Pirie    Éidín Griffin

Sbu's
**Special
Shoes**

These are my big brother
Sbu's shoes.

Look what I can do in them.

I can race cars!

Sometimes, I even race
our bouncy dog.

With Sbu's shoes, I win
every time.

## Wait!

Let me show you
one more thing.

Watch me dance and spin.

I can cartwheel over and over.

I'm a monkey!
Look at me hang
upside down.

Watch me jump
and catch the moon.

Here, try them on!

See what you can do
in Sbu's special shoes.

## The End

There are four seasons in one year. Summer, Fall, Winter and Spring.

It is Winter and it is raining.
Do you enjoy rainy weather?

It is Spring and the
birds are singing.
What happens
in springtime?

291

The four seasons make a year.

Can you name the seasons?

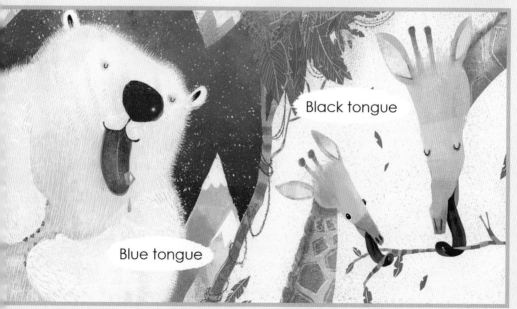

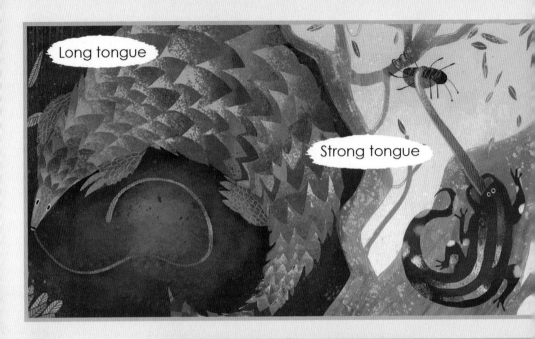

Rough tongue

Smooth tongue

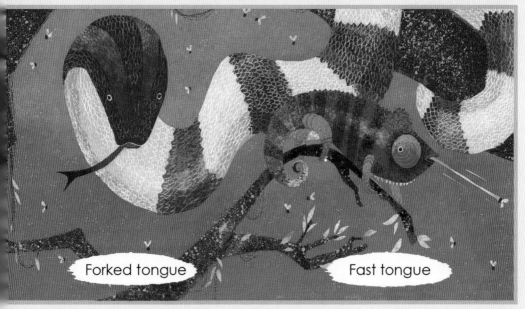

Forked tongue

Fast tongue

Claudi Potter  •  Stephen Wallace  •  Wynand Botha

What is that?
What is that noise?
*Doof-doof-doof*

A cat?
A mouse?
A visitor in the house?

297

No, it's something even
furrier than a cat,
even cuter than a mouse,
and much tinier than you and me.

It's the three Doof-Doofs.
These sweet creatures have
only one foot each to hop on.
And each hop makes a thumping
*doof-doof* on the floor.

Here is Solly Doof, the smart one, who is always thinking looooong and loud. He *uhhs* and *ahhs* and *doof-doofs* all night long.

He reads daytime stories to the other Doof-Doofs, because unlike you and me, that is when they sleep.

Thinky, stinky Solly Doof prefers reading over bathing any time.

Here is Sally Doof, the smallest
and sweetest Doof-Doof of the three.

In a little quiet voice she sings
*doobee-doobee* Doof-Doof songs,
when it gets a bit too quiet in the night.

She likes finding shiny things
and cuddles.

Snuggly, huggly Sally Doof
who loves to sing.

clink clank clunk

Don't forget Silly Doof, the funniest Doof-Doof in the house.

He is always joking.

Wiggly, giggly Silly Doof will make you laugh until your tummy hurts.

He cheers up the other Doof-Doofs whenever they feel sad.

He loves to dance on his big silly foot to the songs that Sally Doof sings.

So, if at night you ever hear a strange *doof-doof* noise again, remember, it's just the three Doof-Doofs, reading, singing and dancing on their one doof-doof foot.

So sleep well, little one. Or keep one eye open ...

Because maybe, just maybe,
you'll see three cute little creatures
hopping past on one foot.

*Doof-doof-doof*

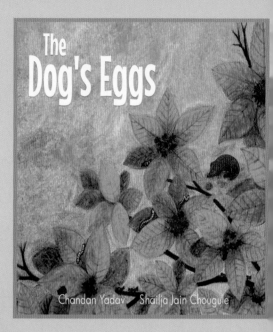

# The
# Dog's Eggs

Chandan Yadav   Shailja Jain Chougule

Mama Bird has laid eggs.

How many eggs do you see?

Mama Bird sits on her eggs.

She keeps them warm.

She sits all day.

She sits all night.

One day, Mama Bird
leaves her nest.

She needs to find food.

Mama Bird sees a dog near her nest.

Oh no!

Will the dog eat my eggs?

He wants to rest in the soft bed!

The dog does not eat the eggs.

The dog takes a nap.

The eggs hatch!

"Mama! Mama!"
say the baby birds.

"Who, me?" says the dog.

"I am not your Mama.
I just took a nap!"

The dog runs away.

The birds run too.

"Stop!" cries Mama Bird.

"That dog is not
your Mama. I am!"

The baby birds come back.

Mama Bird gives them
a big hug.

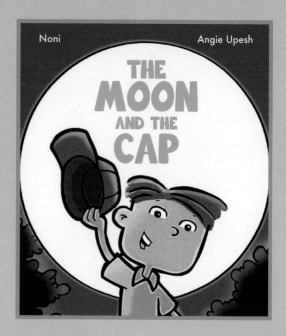

Noni

Angie Upesh

# THE
# MOON
## AND THE
# CAP

We all went
to the fair.

Papa bought Isaac fancy glasses.

Mother bought me a bright blue cap.

The baby got a lollipop.

On the way home, a very strong wind came.

It blew my cap away.

My cap got stuck on a branch of a big old tree.

I cried a lot, and I did not eat my dinner.

Later that night,
the moon came up.

I looked at my cap
in the big old tree.

It tried on my cap.
The moon smiled happily.
I had to smile too.

After school the next day,
my mother gave me a
shiny new red cap.

"The moon sent it," she said.

That night, both the moon
and I wore caps and smiled.
We were happy.

We were happy.

Do you think the sun needs a hat?

Guess which cap I am wearing today!

# The Race

Written by Kanchan Bannerjee
Illustrated by Kavya Singh, Natasha Mehra

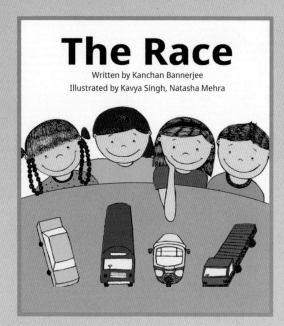

Four friends want to have a race with their toys.

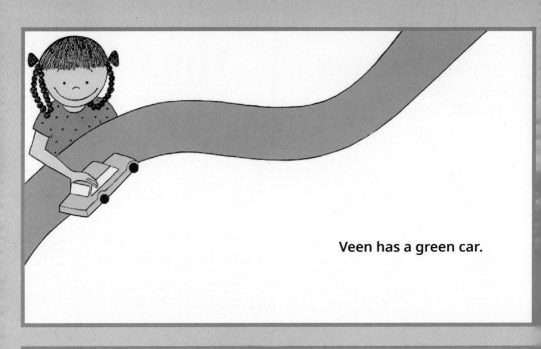

Veen has a green car.

Meena has a yellow car.

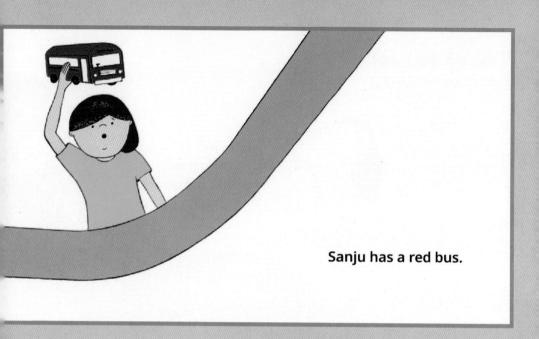

Sanju has a red bus.

Manju has a blue truck.

Ready 1-2-3 ... *GO!*
Here comes Lucky!

Ha ha!
Lucky has
joined the race.

Look, look!
Lucky is the fastest of them all.
Lucky wins the race!

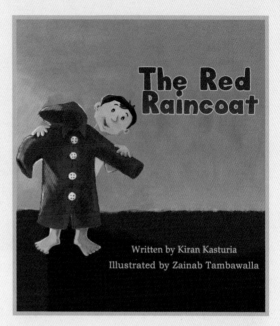

# The Red Raincoat

Written by Kiran Kasturia

Illustrated by Zainab Tambawalla

On Sunday, Manu's parents got him a red raincoat.
"Mama, may I wear it now?" asked Manu.

"No, my dear. The rains are near, but just now the sky is clear," said Mama.

Monday was bright and sunny.
"Will it rain today, Mommy?"
asked Manu.

"No Manu, not today.
If you wear your raincoat, you will
look quite funny!" said Ma.

On Tuesday, the sky was blue.
"Ma, when will my wish come true?"

"Not today, my dear.
There is just one white cloud in the sky!"
said Ma.

Wednesday was hot.
"Mama, why doesn't it rain?" asked Manu.

"Son, I think it will rain very soon.
Maybe even before it's noon," said Mama.

On Thursday, Manu went on a picnic.
"Mama, what if it rains? Should I take
the raincoat with me?" asked Manu.

"No my dear, it will not rain today.
The little white clouds are too
high in the sky," said Mama.

Friday was cloudy.
"Mama, will it rain today?"
asked Manu loudly.

"It might, my dear. There are some
dark clouds low down in the sky,"
said Mama.

Saturday began with a bang!
BADABOOM!

"Mama, is that thunder I hear?
Will it rain very soon?" asked Manu.

And then at last, it started raining!

"Oh, it's raining, it's raining," sang Manu, running out.

"But Manu," called Mama, running after him,

"You forgot your raincoat!"

# Tiger's Delicious Treats

Written by Nguyễn Trần Thiên Lộc

Illustrated by Lê Thị Anh Thư    Translated by Alisha Berger

Tiger lives in a forest.
He loves to bake.

One day, he bakes a delicious batch of green bean pies.

He loads them on a cart and goes to the stream to sell them.

The wind carries the aroma of pies through the air.

The scent reaches Deer,
but he doesn't dare
to follow the scent.

He's scared of Tiger!

It's noon, but Tiger
still hasn't sold a pie.

He returns home
with his cart, disappointed.

That night, Tiger eats all the green bean pies.

His tummy is so full!

The next day,
Tiger bakes a delicious
batch of banana pies.

He goes to sell them
under an ancient tree.

The steam from Tiger's
cart carries the aroma
of the pies up, up, up...

...straight into
Monkey's nose!

Monkey wants to taste
the pies, but doesn't
dare climb down.

He's scared of Tiger.

It's noon, and Tiger hasn't sold any pies.

He returns home with his cart, discouraged.

He eats all the banana pies that night.

His tummy is so, so full!

On the third day,
Tiger bakes delicious
sweet potato pies.

He goes to the meadow
at the edge of the forest
to sell them.

The smell of the sweet
potatoes spreads across
the meadow.

It reaches Pig.

Pig starts feeling hungry.

But Pig is afraid of Tiger!

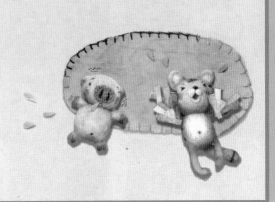

It's noon, but Tiger still hasn't sold any pies.

He returns home with his cart, sadder than ever.

He eats all
the sweet potato pies
that night.

His tummy is now
as big as a balloon!

On the fourth day, Tiger
doesn't bake anything.

He is determined to find
out why nobody is buying
his delicious pies.

He sees Deer, Monkey,
and Pig sitting on
a small hill.

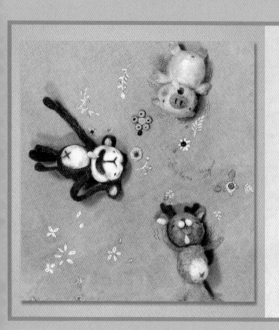

He hears them talking. Monkey says, "Tiger's pies smelled so delicious!"

Pig says, "I'm dying to eat one!"

Deer says, "But we are all afraid of Tiger."

Tiger has an idea!

On the fifth day, Tiger makes three sets of pies: green bean, banana, and sweet potato.

He stuffs them into his biggest cart.

He rolls around in white flour.

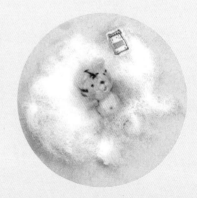

He cuts off his claws.

He puts on a pair
of long ears.

Now Tiger looks like
a Bunny!

He eagerly rolls his cart
to the small hill.

After some time, someone
calls out, "We want to buy
some pies!"

Tiger looks around
and is very surprised.

He sees three tigers
coming to buy his pies!

One tiger has a big nose
and big ears.

One tiger has a pair
of antlers.

One tiger has long arms.

Tiger realizes it's
Pig, Deer and Monkey!

They all recognize Tiger too.

The four of them
burst out laughing.

Nobody is afraid of
Tiger anymore.

They all become friends.

His bakery becomes
the most popular place
in the entire forest.

Every day Tiger sells out
of pies before noon!

# Today was a Noisy Day

Written by Ramya Sriram
Illustrated by Dakshayani Velagapudi

"You must not make any noise today," Mama said.

"Let's see how silent you can be."

"Okay Mama," I said.

"Today, there will be no sound from me!"

I took out my favorite book from the bookshelf and sat down to read.

But I couldn't read because everybody else was making so much noise!

Grandpa was sleeping, but he was also snoring.

Khurrr uhhhh! Khurrr uhhhh!

Grandma was knitting a sweater.

Her bangles went
Clink clink! Clink clink!

Mama turned the page
of her newspaper.

The paper went
Tshhh tshhh! Tshhh tshhh!

Daddy was cooking.
He put onions in the pan.

They went
Fsss Fsss! Fsss Fsss!

The doorbell rang at
our neighbor's house

Ding-dong!
Ding-dong!

A hungry crow was sitting
on the window sill.

It said
Ca-caw! Ca-caw!

I could even hear the big clock
in the hall.

Tick tock!
Tick tock!

Today Mama asked me to be silent, but I heard so many sounds.

I think it was a very noisy day!

348

# Too Big! Too Small!

Written and illustrated by
Lavanya Karthik

"I can't lift you up, Shanu!" says Mom.

**"You are too big!"**

"You can't walk to school alone, Shanu!" says Dad.

**"You are too small!"**

"You can't sleep in the baby's cot, Shanu!" says Grandpa.

**"You are too big!"**

"You can't carry the baby to the park, Shanu!" says Grandma.

**"You are too small!"**

Shanu is puzzled.
**Too big!** Too small!

How can she be too **big** and too small all at once?

Too **big** to wear her old pink dress.

Too small to make pancakes at the stove.

Too **big** to climb up on Grandpa's back?

Too small to carry the baby on hers?

"What am I
the right size for?"
Shanu wonders.

Mom smiles and says,
"Why, you are just
**big** enough to
go to school."

"And you are just small enough for me to carry you on my shoulders," says Dad.

"You are just **big** enough to take me for my morning walks," says Grandpa.

"And you are just small enough for me to tell stories to," says Grandma.

"And you will always, always be the **perfect** size ... for this!" they all say, and give her a warm, wonderful hug.

# Tumi Goes to the Park

Nyambura Kariuki   Hannah Shone   Paballo Rampa

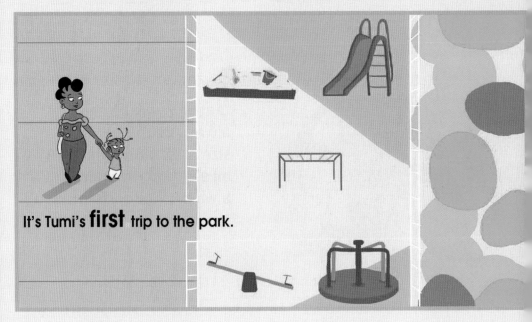

It's Tumi's **first** trip to the park.

"Mama, **what's that?**"
"It's a slide," says Mama.

"May I go on it?" asks Tumi.
"Of course!" says Mama.

"Wheeeee!"

"Look Mama, I swing like a

**monkey.**"

"I just went past you
**ten times,**
Mama!" says Tumi.

"Clever girl!"
says Mama.
"You know
how to
count!"

Tumi sees the sandpit.

**"Let's build a sandcastle!"**

says Tumi.

"I'm taking a photo for Gogo," says Mama.

"It's time to go home now, Tumi," says Mama.

**"Bye, Zakhe!"** waves Tumi.

**"Bye, Tumi!"** says Zahke. "See you next time!"

361

"Mama, **thank you** for bringing me to the park," says Tumi.

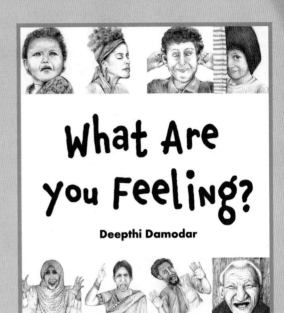

# What Are you Feeling?

**Deepthi Damodar**

## Sad

**Angry**

**Scared**

**Joyous**

**Surprised**

**Playful**

**Peaceful**

# Shy

WHAT IS IT?

"La-La, La, La,
La, La, La ..."

"Is that sound coming
from everywhere?"
"Is it coming from
somewhere?"
"It is coming from there!"

"La-La, La, La,
La, La, La ..."

"Is it from the sky?"
"Is is from the tree?"
"It is from the bush!"

"La-La, La, La,
La, La, La ..."

"Is it black?"

"Is it white?"

"It is brown!"

"La-La, La, La, La, La, La ..."

"Is it a prayer?"

"It is a poem?"

"It is a song!"

"Is it a cuckoo?"

"Is it a mynah bird?"

"La-La, La, La,
La, La, La ..."

"It is a donkey!"

"It is a donkey!"

"It is a donkey! Sing on!"

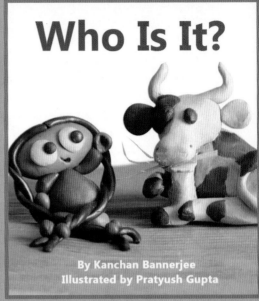

# Who Is It?

By Kanchan Bannerjee
Illustrated by Pratyush Gupta

Priya hears a sound.

**Srrr ... Srrr ...**

Who is it?

Priya runs out.

She sees the cow chewing grass.

No, it is not the cow that is making the sound.

Is it the monkey in the tree?

No, it is not the monkey.

Is it the frog
hopping in the grass?

No, it is not the frog.

Is it the deer
jumping along?

No, it is not the deer.

Is it the fish in the pond?

No, it is not the fish.

Then Priya sees
the elephant!

The elephant is rubbing
its back against a tree.

Now Priya has her answer!

**Srrr ... Srrr ...**

# Who Is Our Friend?

By Jade Mathieson
Illustrated by Gerhard Van Wyk

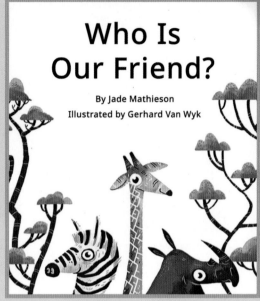

Can you guess who our best friend is?
**He's not like us at all.**

Our best friend is **bird.**

I am Rhino.
**I get covered in fleas.**

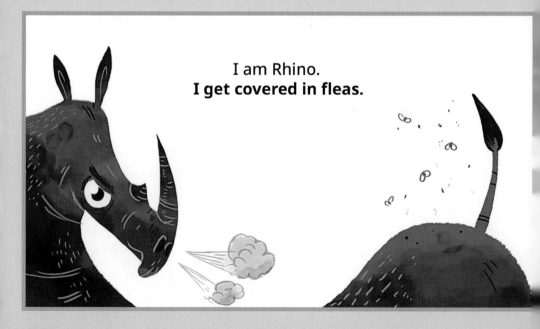

Bird eats them all up.

I am Crocodile.
**I can't brush my teeth.**

Bird pecks them all clean.

I am Giraffe.
**I can't scratch my head.**

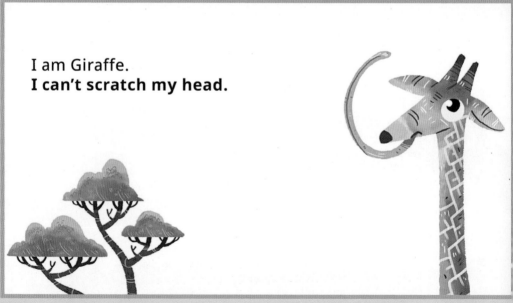

Bird can reach just the right spot.

I am Zebra.
**I can't see things far away.**

Bird has great eyes,
**so when he's watching,
I'm safe.**

Bird might be different,
but that's no problem ...

We don't even mind when he sings!

# Whose Button Is This?

Tinny Tim was sitting on the road when a button bounced his way.

"I wonder where this comes from," he said. He wanted to find out.

It was busy on the side of the road.

"Woah!"

He nearly got squashed.

He made a lucky escape.

"It's scary out here," he said.

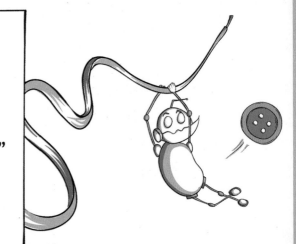

"Hey there, is this yours?"

The green man said nothing. He just turned red.

"What a rude person."

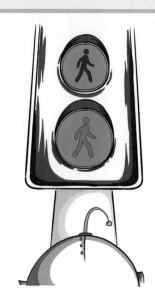

Tinny Tim carried on looking.

"Whose button is this?"

"Woah..!

...at least he's friendly."

"I've got to get to the other side. I'm sure that's where this comes from."

SPLASH!

"That was close."

He waited for the cars to pass before he carried on.

Maybe this was who he was looking for.

"Hello, who are you?"

"I'm Ruby Rags."

"I think this is yours," he said.

"Thank you, little robot. Can we be friends?"

# Wiggle Jiggle

Megan Vermaak, Mathapelo Mabaso,
and Chenel Ferreira

# Wiggle
## jiggle
### wriggle!

I am a wiggly
caterpillar.

Flowers and leaves are my favorite food.

Yummy in my tummy!

Wiggle jiggle wriggle!

I am a wiggly caterpillar.

I love the rain.
**Pitter-patter**
on the leaves.

Watch me
wiggle and dance.
**Wiggle**
*jiggle*
wriggle!

395

Poop!

My magic poop makes plants grow BIG.

I love to see my plants grow.
Yellow, red, blue, and green.

Wiggle *jiggle* wriggle!

I am a wiggly caterpillar.

Wiggle when you see me in the garden.

Wiggle *jiggle* wriggle!

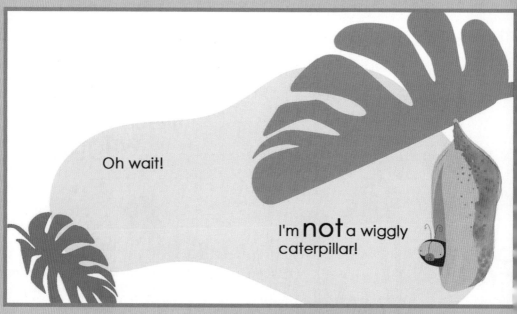

# Flitter

## flutter

### flitter!

I am a butterfly!

# WILD CAT! WILD CAT!

WRITTEN BY SEJAL MEHTA
ILLUSTRATED ROHAN CHAKRAVARTY

Some wild cats have stripes.

Like the **tiger!**

Some wild cats have manes.                    Like the **lion**!

Some wild cats have spots.          Like the **leopard** and the **leopard cat**!

Some wild cats are the best climbers.

Like the **clouded leopard** and the **marbled cat**!

Some wild cats live high up in the mountains.

Like the **snow leopard** and the **Pallas's cat**!

Some wild cats live in the desert.          Like the **desert cat!**

Some wild cats have hairy ears.          Like the **caracal** and the **lynx!**

Some wild cats love to fish.

Like the **fishing cat**!

Some wild cats are
the smallest wild cats in the world.

Like the **rusty-spotted cat**!

Some wild cats look like house cats.

Like the **jungle cat**
and the **golden cat**!

But they are all wild cats!

**Don't be scared.**

**Woof-woof out!**

Look, Doggy's bringing the ball.

Ball?

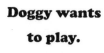

Doggy wants
to play.

Play?

Catch the ball.

**Now you play.**

**Catch, Woof-woof!**

**The End.**

# Attributions

*A Beautiful Day* (English) written by Elana Bregin, illustrated by Lindy Pelzl. Originally published by Book Dash. Copyright © 2014 Book Dash. Licensed under a CC BY 4.0 license on StoryWeaver.

*A House for a Mouse* (English) written by Michele Fry, illustrated by Amy Uzzell. Originally published by Book Dash. Copyright © 2014 Book Dash. Licensed under a CC BY 4.0 license on StoryWeaver.

*Abdul the Octopus* (English) written by Mamta D, illustrated by Muniza Shariq, Nikhila Anil, Rajiv Eipe, Samidha Gunjal, & Thea Nicole de Klerk. Copyright © 2018 Mamta D. Licensed under a CC BY 4.0 license on StoryWeaver. Text changes: p. 3: added 'Where do you live?' p. 4: added 'How many do you have?' p. 5: added 'to hide.' p. 6: 'marine life' changed to 'sea creatures.' p. 7: 'Want to see an Octopus? Visit an aquarium' changed to 'Would you like to meet me? Maybe someday you will!'.

*Animal Homes*, originally titled *Houses of Animals* HOUSES OF ANIMALS (English) translated by Anirudh Prakhya from జంతువుల ఇళ్ళు (English-Telugu), by Ashwitha Jayakumar. Based on the original story Animal Homes (English) written by Ashwitha Jayakumar, and illustrated by Nafisa Nandini Crishna. Copyright © 2020 Anirudh Prakhya. Originally published by Pratham Books. Licensed under a CC BY 4.0 license on StoryWeaver. Text changes: p. 3: 'houses' changed to 'homes up' and 'That's all for the bees too' changed to 'And so do bees.' p. 4: 'roam' changed to 'spin' and 'taller houses' to 'tall, tall homes.' p. 6: 'while frogs live in the water, even on the ground' changed to 'Frogs can live in water and on land.' p. 7: 'roost under the ground' changed to 'live in burrows under the ground.' p. 8: 'Chimpanzees turn their trees into houses' changed to 'Apes make trees their homes.' p. 9: 'foxes live in caves' changed to 'wolves live in dens' p. 10: 'are in marshy places' changed to 'live in swamps.' p. 11: changed to 'Deer live in forests and so do tigers!' p. 12: changed to 'Some animals live close to us and some live far away. But do you know what we have in common with all the animals of the world? We all build our homes in one large home...Planet Earth!'.

*Ayaan and the Fox* (English) written by Right To Play, illustrated by Sonal Goyal & Sumit Sakhuja. Copyright © 2019 Right To Play. Licensed under a CC BY 4.0 license on StoryWeaver.

*Bow Meow Wow* (English) written and illustrated by Priya Kuriyan. Copyright © 2018 Pratham Books. Originally published by Pratham Books. Licensed under a CC BY 4.0 license on StoryWeaver.

*Bugs by Numbers* written and illustrated by Danielle Bruckert. Copyright © 2010 Danielle Bruckert. Originally published by Red Sky Ventures. Licensed under a CC BY 4.0 license. Text changes: p. 9: deleted 'on the rock.' p. 17: deleted 'Each ladybug has three black dots on each side of their backs, can you see?'.

*Busy Ants* (English) written by Kanchan Bannerjee, illustrated by Deepa Balsavar. Copyright © 2015 Pratham Books. Originally published by Pratham Books. Licensed under a CC BY 4.0 license on StoryWeaver.

*Clever Pig* (English) written by Nathalie Koenig, illustrated by Josh Morgan. Copyright © 2016 Book Dash. Originally published by Book Dash Licensed under a CC BY 4.0 license on StoryWeaver.

*Colors!* (English) translated by Lea Shaver from ولكيام ناولأ (Arabic) by Justin Amey. Copyright © Lea Shaver, 2018. Based on the original story Meiko's Colors (English) written by Justin Amey, illustrated by Jesse Breytenbach. Licensed under a CC BY 4.0 license on StoryWeaver. Text changes: p. 8: added 'Her dress.' p. 18: added 'The End'.

*Colors in the Wild*, originally titled *Colours in the Wild* (English) written by Menaka Raman, illustrated by Anita Mani, Nanditha Chandraprakash, Rajiv Eipe, Rohit Varma, Sambath Subbaiah, & Vipul Ramanuj. Copyright © 2017 Menaka Raman. Licensed under a CC BY 4.0 license on StoryWeaver. Text changes: p. 3: changed 'brown' to 'gray'.

*Colors of Nature*, originally titled *Colours of Nature* (English), written by Bulbul Sharma, illustrated by Bulbul Sharma. Copyright © 2006 Pratham Books. Originally published by Pratham Books. Licensed under a CC BY 4.0 license on StoryWeaver.

*Come Stay With Me* (English) written by Nasrin Siege, illustrated by Subi Bosa. Copyright © 2019 Book Dash. Originally published by Book Dash. Licensed under a CC BY 4.0 license on StoryWeaver. Text changes: p. 6: 'come stay with me' changed to 'you can come stay with me, Tendai' p. 14: added 'the next day'.

*Counting Animals* (English) written by Clare Verbeek, Thembani Dladla, & Zanele Buthelezi; illustrated by Rob Owen. Copyright © 2007 African Storybook Initiative. Originally published by African Storybook Initiative. Licensed under a CC BY 4.0 license on StoryWeaver.

*Friends* (English) written by Hlengiwe Zondi & Zimbili Dlamini, illustrated by Catherine Groenewald. Copyright © 2014 African Storybook Initiative. Originally published by African Storybook Initiative. Licensed under a CC BY 4.0 license on StoryWeaver.

*Grandpa Farouk's Garden* (English) written by Matthew Kalil, illustrated by Sam van Riet. Copyright © 2018 Book Dash. Originally published by Book Dash. Licensed under a CC BY 4.0 license on StoryWeaver. Text changes: all instances of 'ladybirds' changed to 'ladybugs' p. 2: deleted 'surrounded by houses and brick and tar.' added 'is where' p. 5: deleted 'and works with his Grandpa all day' added 'too' p. 6: deleted 'when they

414

finish they' added 'when all the work in the garden is done, Amir and Grandpa' p. 8: deleted. p. 9: added '"My garden is unwell" says Grandpa. "Look closely. Tiny pests are eating the plants" says Grandpa' p. 10: deleted 'said Grandpa. "They are the pests that eat bugs that kill the plants. Without ladybirds the garden will die." added 'They will eat up all the pests!' p. 11: 'I'll bring you a bug or two' changed to 'I can bring you ladybugs' p. 12: deleted 'For a whole week, Amir looked and searched and collected' added 'And he does!' p. 13: 'he found' changed to 'Amir finds' p. 14: deleted 'two more' p. 17: changed to 'Amir takes the ladybugs to Grandpa Farouk. "Well done! You found 10 ladybugs!" says Grandpa' p. 18: deleted 'were very hungry' added 'fly into the garden' p. 19: deleted 'the ladybirds ate the pests' p. 2:0 changed to 'The garden is full of flowers again. "Thank you, ladybugs!" says Amir'.

# The Learning
# Journey
### Starts Here

# AILA™
## Sit & Play

## Virtual Preschool

AILA Sit & Play provides an essential and robust early preschool curriculum covering ABCs, 123s, colors, shapes, words, reading, and music for your child at home or in the classroom.

## Personal Teacher

AILA adapts to your child's unique learning style while managing screen time and delivering the right content at the right time.

## Safe Companion

AILA offers hands-free and worry-free exclusive content without ads or inappropriate subjects. There are no subscription fees and all updates are FREE.

## Daily Learning Adventures

Adorable original characters encourage your child to talk, read, count, sing, dance, and play games for a happy child at home or on the go.